W9-AOQ-848

❧ THE ❧
CHRISTMAS PUPPY

✿ THE ✿
CHRISTMAS PUPPY

by Roberta Grobel Intrater
Illustrations by Bruce McNally

Cartwheel
·B·O·O·K·S· ®

SCHOLASTIC INC.
New York Toronto London Auckland Sydney
Mexico City New Delhi Hong Kong

ISBN 0-439-14256-3

12 11 10 9 8   2 3 4/0

Printed in the U.S.A.   23

First Scholastic club printing, November 1999

For Zach,
who always makes the right choices.
—R.G.I.

To my wife, Nikky.
—B.M.

chapter one

Nobody knows where Tina was born or even who her parents were. She just showed up at the shelter one day and so did we. She was curled up like a ball, almost lost in all the newspapers on the bottom of her cage. But as soon as she

saw me, she raced over, pressed her nose through the wire, and tried to give me a kiss. I knew right then she was the one we were taking home.

Mom laughed and Grandma said she was the teeniest thing she'd ever seen. That's how she got her name—Tina, because she looked so teeny.

She was a beautiful puppy with short tan and white hair. Her face was white, with tan patches around her soft brown eyes. Her paws and belly and the tip of her tail were white, too, but her floppy ears were all tan.

The lady at the shelter opened the cage and put her in my arms. Tina rubbed her soft little head against my neck, then laid it on my shoulder.

"Uh-oh!" my mom said when she petted her. "She's a shedder. She's going to shed all over our clothes." But I just held Tina real tight and gave Mom that look. "She'll make a mess out of the house," Mom said to my grandma. "We'd better look for a poodle or an Airedale. I don't want a dog that sheds."

"But just look at them together," Grandma said, as I squeezed my eyebrows together till I looked pitiful. "They both have the same sad eyes." I love when my grandmother comes with us. She really understands.

So Mom made a donation to the shelter and they gave us training books and a red collar with a leash that matched. We put Tina in the car, but instead of going right home, we headed for my aunt Helen's house. It was Memorial Day weekend and Aunt Helen was having a barbecue for the whole family. Tina and I were pretty tired, so we snuggled together in the back seat. Just before we fell asleep, Mom turned around and smiled.

"Look at how she nestled right in there," I heard her say to Grandma. "She really is adorable. Such a calm little puppy."

It's amazing how often my Mom can be wrong. It didn't take long to find out how wrong she was this time.

❧❧❧

Everyone was surprised when we arrived with Tina. So were we. We'd

forgotten about Ripper, my cousin
Carol's mean little poodle. As soon
as he saw us, he jumped up, knocking
the bowl of potato salad out of Aunt
Helen's arms. He started barking
at Tina as pieces of potato flew
everywhere. They landed on the walls,
the floor, the chairs, and even in Aunt
Helen's hair!

Ripper raced around, eating all the
potato salad he could find. Tina got
nervous and wet the floor. Mom ran to
get some paper towels as Uncle Ben came
storming into the hallway.

"What's going on here?" he growled.

"Look at my puppy, Uncle Ben,"
I said, trying to keep him from noticing
the puddle on the floor.

"Hmmmm," he muttered. He sounded pretty annoyed, but he petted Tina on the head.

"She'll be fine," Mom told him as she mopped up the floor. "We'll put her in the yard. That'll keep her out of the way."

Just then, the doorbell rang. Tina raced toward the door. It was my dad.

"What's this?" Dad asked, as Tina pulled on his shoelaces. "Where did you come from?"

"No one really knows," I said, "but isn't she cute?"

"Sure is," Dad said. Then he turned to my uncle. "When did you get her?"

"She's ours, Dad," I told him.

He got a strange look on his face. "Ours?" he said slowly.

"Well," Mom said, "I told you we were going to pick up my mother and that on the way back we might stop at the shelter…"

"'Just to have a look' is what you said," Dad replied. And then, just when I thought he was going to get angry, he picked Tina up and she licked his nose.

"She's a real cutie," he said as he placed her back on the floor. I saw him smile as he watched her run in circles, chasing her own tail.

"Let's get ready to eat," someone said. We all headed out to the backyard. That's when we heard the crash.

Everyone rushed back to the kitchen. There was Tina, covered in cole slaw and nibbling on a raw hamburger. She'd

pulled the tablecloth off the kitchen table and our whole dinner along with it! There were chicken legs and hot dogs and beans all over the place. What a mess!

"I hope you all like tuna fish," said Grandpa. He was always trying to be funny. Then Ripper started to nip at everyone's feet because he couldn't get past the crowd at the doorway. My uncle started yelling some of those words you're not supposed to say around grandparents and kids. That's when my father decided to treat everyone to dinner at the nearest restaurant.

"But where will we leave Tina?" I asked.

"In the basement," he grumbled. Then he leaned closer to Mom and I heard him whisper, "This dog of yours has just cost us $300 bucks and we haven't even had her one day!"

chapter two

That was just the beginning. Tina, it turned out, was always getting into trouble. One day, she ate up the insides of my mom's favorite shoes. She took them out of the closet and chewed up the linings. Then, real carefully, she put them right back where she found them.

Another time, she got hold of my toothpaste and toothbrush. She ate the brush and squeezed the toothpaste all over the rug.

Dad said he couldn't take her to his workshop anymore because she chewed up the leg of a table he was building for a client. And Mom caught Tina under her drawing table, happily eating colored markers. Tina's coat was red, yellow and blue and the floor was a scribbled mess.

"Lucky you didn't touch the drawing I was working on, Tina!" I heard Mom yelling from her studio. "Or *you'd* have to call the magazine and tell them what happened to their illustrations!"

A dog making a phone call? Tina really pushed Mom over the edge that time.

She was full of mischief, but we loved her a lot. Even my mom. She soon stopped complaining about how Tina shed all over everything and was ruining the whole house with her chewing. She even stopped complaining when Tina had a little "accident" on the rug, but that happened less and less as Tina got older.

And Dad got used to waking up at 6:00 every morning because Tina would lick his face until he got out of bed to walk her.

I used to hate going to bed until Tina came along. She always made it seem like fun. She'd race me to the room, jump on the bed, curl up against my legs, and keep me warm until I fell asleep. Then, as soon as she heard my parents climb the stairs, she'd dash into their room and warm their bed up, too. Tina slept with all of us—but she only stole the covers from my dad.

She had become a real member of our family. She was even turning into a good watch dog. Whenever a stranger came to the door, she'd jump up and down and bark like crazy. Mom said she was finally growing up. But Tina had one very bad habit.

She loved to escape from the yard. Mom started to call her Houdina, after that famous magician named Houdini, who could escape from anywhere. We had a wooden fence all around our yard. It seemed pretty tall until the day we saw Tina tip her head, take a good look at it and start to run. Before we could stop her, she flew over the top, graceful as a bird.

We built a higher fence, but she just dug a hole and went under it. Dad filled the hole with big rocks and put chicken wire along the bottom. Then Tina discovered the gate. She jumped up, pushing her nose against the hook until it came out of its catch. So we added a long latch. She kept trying to find another escape route.

Most of the time, we'd manage to keep Tina in the yard. We didn't worry about it too much. Whenever she did get out, Tina always came home soon. "That Houdina!" Mom said with a chuckle. "She just loves to run free."

One day, we went to visit my grandparents. They lived pretty far away. After we all had lunch together, Grandpa decided he needed some exercise. He grabbed Tina's leash and took her for a walk.

While they were out, Tina pulled real hard on the leash and managed to break free. Poor Grandpa. He wanted exercise, but not this much. He started running

after her, but he couldn't keep up. He got back to the house, out of breath and very upset.

"She ran like the wind," he said. "I'm afraid I lost her."

We all ran out of the house to look for Tina. Grandma and Grandpa took their car and Mom and Dad took ours.

We drove through the streets with our heads hanging out the windows, shouting "Tina! Tina!" But she didn't answer our calls.

When we got back, I locked myself in the bathroom, sat down on the edge of the tub, and cried and cried. I was sure I'd never see her again.

About a half hour later we heard Tina barking. She was standing on the front steps, waiting to be let in, as if nothing had happened.

"That dog has a built-in compass," said Grandpa. He was so happy to see Tina that he hugged her hard. "Look at how she found her way back," he said, sounding really proud. "And this is the first time she's ever been here!"

There was never a dull moment with Tina around. She loved to knock the phone off the hook when it rang and bark into the receiver. Or dig up Mom's favorite geraniums and lay them at her feet. One day, she took off after a squirrel and tried to climb the tree. The squirrel raced to the top of the branches, but Tina didn't give up. When she finally stopped jumping, her identification tags were missing.

"That dog!" said my mom. "That's the second set of tags she's lost. I'm going to go broke keeping her in dog tags and rawhide bones! And she's eating us out of house and home."

It was true. Tina would eat anything, anytime, anywhere. She'd bark if my mom had a cup of coffee and didn't share it with her. We had to mix her dried food with milk for breakfast and chicken soup for dinner. She even ate a lemon once, skin and all. She sure was a funny dog. And the funnier she was, the more we loved her. Every day was a new adventure and she always made us laugh. She fit right into our family.

All summer long, Tina and I played together. I taught her to catch a frisbee, and she loved to interrupt when my friends and I tossed a tennis ball around. She'd jump up and grab it and make it all soggy, and then she'd try to bury it before we caught up with her. All the kids loved Tina. She was so much fun.

chapter three

Soon summer turned into fall and I had to go back to school. Tina and I didn't have as much time to spend together anymore, but she was always waiting at the door to greet me when I got home. The weather grew colder and the leaves began to turn color. At the end of September, my dad started to make a big fuss about turning forty. Mom was already planning a surprise party to celebrate his birthday.

Mom and Grandma and Aunt Helen cooked for days. We got some of Dad's friends to take him bowling, and then we decorated the house with balloons and streamers. Two of Dad's brothers were in a band and they all showed up to play. Dad was in complete shock when he came home and saw everyone crammed into the living room. He looked like he'd just swallowed a live fish!

Everyone was having a great time and Tina was on her best behavior. She didn't bark or run around too much. But one of the neighbors, a grumpy woman named Martha, said she saw Tina eat a stuffed grape leaf.

"She took it right off that dish on the cocktail table," she insisted. "I saw her tongue right on it!"

"That's ridiculous," Mom told her. "Everyone knows dogs don't eat grape leaves. They eat meat." Mom winked at me and kept on talking. "Look at her, she's sitting so nicely. Good girl, Tina."

Tina *was* sitting nicely, with her pink tongue hanging out, looking sweet and innocent. Mom passed the grape leaves around but only Stanley, the math teacher, took one. Stanley was like Tina. He'd eat anything.

"Well," said Martha in a loud voice, "I really think you ought to put that dog outside."

Everybody was starting to look over that way. Mom sort of rolled her eyes and took a deep breath. Then she looked at Tina and said gently, "Okay, girl. How about a little fresh air?"

Tina jumped up and ran to the back door. Mom let her out. Then the band started to play "Happy Birthday" and Mom lit the candles on the cake. We all got so involved in singing and eating and opening presents that we forgot Tina was outside.

The party went on pretty late and my friends and I stayed up playing video games and stuffing our faces with junk food. It was terrific. Nobody noticed how cold it had gotten until people started to leave.

When we opened the door, a strong wind rushed in. Leaves had fallen off the trees and were whipping around the yard. A light snow started to fall, which was really weird for September. All the guests raced to their cars, laughing and shouting about the crazy weather and how they'd probably have to ski to work the next day. Dad said he'd better get out his winter jacket to take Tina for a walk.

He whistled, but she didn't come. Then he called her name, but she still didn't come. That's when Mom remembered that she'd put her outside in the yard. We all went out back to look for her, but Tina wasn't there. She had never left the yard at night before. But this night was different.

"She's not wearing any tags," Mom remembered. The new ones she'd ordered hadn't arrived yet. "I should have made a cardboard name tag with our phone number," she said sadly.

"I should have double-checked the gate," said Dad.

"But she always comes back," I said. "Don't you think she'll come back tonight?"

"I sure hope so," said Dad. "We'll leave the gate open and keep the yard light on. Tina's not the type to lose her way."

We watched and we waited, but she didn't show up.

I stayed up real late that night. I remember watching my mom, standing alone and staring out the window. The snow was piling up. It was thick and

white. Great packing snow—the kind I always get so happy about. But not this time. This time, all I could think about was Tina, outside, on her own. I walked over to my mom and put my hand in hers.

"She'll sleep on someone's porch," I said. *Unless she ran to the park*, I thought to myself. But I couldn't stand to think about that. Poor Tina. How would she keep warm?

⌒⌒⌒

The next day was just as bad. I went to school, but I couldn't concentrate. Dad went to his shop, but he didn't get much done. And Mom went to the offices of the magazine she worked for, but she forgot to take the envelope with all her drawings in it. After school, I made posters with Tina's picture pasted in the center and hung them all around the neighborhood.

Grandma called. "She's so pretty and friendly," she said. "Someone must have picked her up and taken her out of the cold. Someone who loves animals."

"If she were outside," Grandpa said, "she would have come home by now. She has a built-in compass, remember?"

It didn't help. I didn't feel any better. None of us did.

Friends called. "That crazy dog," they'd say to Mom, trying to cheer her up. "Maybe you're better off. You'll get a dog you can train next time." Mom would shake her head and hang up.

"They just don't understand," she said, tears filling her eyes. "Tina fit. She fit into our lives and we loved her. She was part of our family."

We sent letters to all the vets in town and stapled more posters to the trees. Neighbors read the signs and called. "How sad. We hope you find her." Kids saw the reward we were offering and rang our bell. "Wow! Fifty bucks! I'm going to look for that dog. I think I saw her yesterday."

⸎

One afternoon, after Tina had been gone almost a week, Mom saw a dog with short blond hair and white paws standing in front of our house. "Tina! Tina!" she yelled.

I was so excited, I nearly tripped over the wires of my computer as I raced to the door.

"Tina!" I cried, pushing past Mom. The dog turned around. It had a thick brown collar around its neck. There were no patches around its eyes. It was not Tina at all.

We got a lot of phone calls that night. We asked everyone the same question. They all gave the same answer. The dog they saw was wearing a thick brown collar.

A few weeks went by. We started to adjust to life without Tina. It was a little quieter, a lot duller, and much more lonely. But we were getting used to it. We even thought about getting another puppy, but we just couldn't bring ourselves to do that yet. We were sure that if she were living with someone in the neighborhood, old Houdina would find a way to escape back to her home. Mom figured the only reason she hadn't come home was because she must have found another family who loved her as much as we did.

chapter four

The weather got a little colder and then winter finally set in. Our family had a huge Thanksgiving dinner and then we started to get ready for Christmas.

Late one afternoon, Mom asked me to go shopping with her to help pick out some presents for the family. That was fine with me. I knew she really wanted to see what I liked for myself, so she could surprise me with the perfect gift. I was feeling pretty cheerful until she added the bad part.

"Zach," she said, "you're growing like a weed. Your pants are so short they're touching the tops of your socks! It's time to get new ones."

There's nothing in the world I hate more than shopping for clothes with my mom. She insists that I try everything on. It takes a tremendous amount of yelling and jumping around to make her realize that I won't. She tries to pull the clothes on me. I push back and holler. Finally, she gives up and buys a bunch of things that

I won't wear anyway. I don't know why she always insists on taking me along. When it comes to shopping, my mom's harder to train than Tina.

We always go downtown to buy clothes. That's fine with me, too, since I wouldn't want to run into any of my friends while I'm in the middle of a clothes shopping tantrum.

Mom's favorite place is Karl's Kute Kids' Klothes. Nothing could be worse than being seen walking into that dumb store. The name isn't even spelled right. All of my friends go to the mall, but Mom always says, "Karl's got great bargains on good quality clothes." As if I really cared. He doesn't have any cool stuff, and besides, it's embarrassing to shop in a place called Kute Kids' Klothes. I hate that place.

You can't just walk into Karl's. Karl has to buzz you in. Every time he sees me at the door, he hides behind the counter and pretends not to hear the bell. He called me the "Tantrum King" once. Mom just doesn't get it. "If that man is deaf," she always says, "then why does he have a buzzer system? Why doesn't he just leave the door open?" Then she rings and rings until one of his salesmen finally comes to the door.

I always smile nicely at Karl. Actually, it's more like a laugh without a sound. He knows and I know and Mom knows (even though she pretends she doesn't) what's coming next: my tantrums are hard to forget. But this time it was different. This time we never made it to the store. Because this time, we saw Tina.

She was wearing a gold collar that looked like it was decorated with diamonds. It was too fancy, but it actually looked pretty good on her. At the other end of her long leash was a scruffy old man in a worn coat. He looked like he hadn't shaved in a week.

"Tina!" I screamed at the top of my lungs. Mom slammed the car to a halt.

"Where?" she asked.

"There!" I shouted, pointing. Just then Tina noticed us and started to bark. She was jumping so wildly that the old man could hardly hold her down.

"Princess!" he yelled. When he opened his mouth, I could see he was missing some teeth. "Princess! Hey! Quiet down, girl."

I jumped out of the car and so did Mom. We ran over to Tina and started hugging and kissing her, right there in the middle of Broadway. Tina kissed us, too. The old man kept saying, "Calm down, Princess, calm down."

Then my mom stood up to face the man and held out her hand. "I can see that you took very good care of our dog and I want to thank you for that." The old man just looked at her as though she were crazy.

"That's my dog, lady," he said, "and we got to get going now."

The man scratched Tina's ears and she wagged her tail at him. Then he tugged on the leash and started to lead her away.

"Wait a minute!" Mom shouted. "You can't do this!" But the man kept walking. "I'll get the police," she yelled as she ran down the street after him. "That's our dog!"

A bunch of people stopped to watch what was happening. "That's our dog!" I shouted after the old man. "Tina! Tina!" I called.

Tina was looking back at us the whole time, jumping and choking in her shiny collar. My mom caught up with the man and grabbed his arm.

"Stop!" she commanded in her best no-nonsense voice. And he did. I couldn't believe it. The old guy actually stopped moving. Then he knelt down and put his arms around Tina.

He looked up at my mom and said, in a shaky voice, "Listen, lady, she's the only family I got. You got that nice boy over there and maybe a husband and a house and lots of family and friends. I just got Princess here. We found each other, see? Saved each other, you might say.

"Remember that freak snowstorm in September? I woulda froze to death on a park bench if she hadn't come along and woke me up. I took her home with me and gave her some dinner. Right girl?" He turned to Tina and she licked his stubbly face.

"She saved me and I saved her and I ain't about to give her up." He patted Tina on the head and stood up. "I ain't givin' you up, Princess," he said softly. "You can count on me."

Nobody said anything for a minute. My mom looked like she was thinking real hard. She looked kind of sad, too. As for me, I just started to cry. Right there, in the middle of Broadway, with all those people staring at us.

"She's *my* dog," I said to the old man. "And I love her. We paid to get her at the shelter and we took her to the vet for all her shots and bought her toys even though she ate up our shoes and..."

The old man stopped me right there. "Well then," he said, "maybe this ain't your dog after all, because she never ate any of *my* shoes."

"You probably only have one pair," I mumbled, even though I knew it was kind of mean.

"That's right, sonny," he said. "That's all I got and she had the good sense not to eat 'em."

"Well, that's because she's not a little puppy anymore," I told him. I knew a thing or two about dogs.

"Nope," he said, "she ain't a baby. She's a grown-up pup. And healthy, too. I take good care of her. Some days, she eats better than I do."

"She eats a lot, doesn't she?" I asked.

"Eats me out of house and home," he said.

"That's what my mom used to say. Isn't it, Mom?" I could feel myself smiling at him. Maybe this old guy wasn't so bad after all. Maybe if I was nice to him, he'd just hand me the leash and go away. Or maybe he'd go away if we gave him the reward. He looked like he could use the money.

"There's a $50 reward for finding her," I told him. Then I turned to Mom. "Give him the reward, Mom," I said. "That's what he wants."

"No, it isn't," she said. "And I think you know that too, Zach."

"Look," the old man said, hugging Tina even tighter, "we're happy together. See how good she looks. You said it yourself. And she's well-behaved, too. I trained her good. Watch this."

He told Tina to lie down and she did it right away. He dropped the leash and said, "Stay" and she didn't move an inch, not even when I called her. She just sat there and watched his hand. Then he said roll over, and she rolled over, as smooth as a ball. He moved his finger and whispered, "Come" and she ran over to him. He reached inside his pocket and took out a milk bone. Tina didn't jump up to get it. She sat calmly until he put it in her mouth.

"Good girl, Princess," he said gently, as he patted her on the head. I couldn't believe my eyes. Maybe it wasn't the same dog. But of course, it was. She knew us. She knew her old name. She was bigger, but she had the same patches around her eyes and a white spot on the tip of her tail. It was Tina all right, but not the same funny puppy that was always getting into trouble. This was a new Tina. Somehow, this old man had taught her how to behave and she seemed to like it.

I looked at them together. The old man had such a proud expression on his face and Tina sat up so straight, looking at him and wagging her tail. I had to admit, they really seemed like a team. Mom was right. Tina had found someone else who loved her as much as we did.

chapter five

It was starting to get dark and the
lights decorating the stores began
to glow brightly. All around us, people
were rushing home, carrying shopping
bags filled with presents. A man walked
past us, dragging a Christmas tree.

I remember the sweet smell of roasting peanuts and a song about chestnuts on an open fire coming from one of the stores. The cold air suddenly felt very warm. As warm as the inside of our house on Christmas Eve.

I looked into the old man's eyes. "She's the only family I got," I heard him say once more. Only his lips weren't moving. I heard it again, over and over in my mind. *She's the only family I got.*

Then I heard a bark. Two police officers had moved through the crowd of people who were watching us. The lady cop put her hand on the old man's arm. Tina pressed herself against the old man's leg and began to growl.

The other cop looked at me. "Is this your dog, son?" he asked. "Did this man steal your dog?" Tina kept guarding the old man, baring her teeth and growling.

"No, no," Mom said quickly.
"He didn't steal her. There's been
some mistake."

"Well," the lady cop said, "we had
a report that an old man down on
Broadway had stolen a boy's dog."

"No, officers," Mom said, "he found
the dog. That's all."

"Okay," the lady cop said to the
old man, as she let go of his arm. "Now
why don't you just give him back. Go
on. Give that nice young boy over
there his leash."

"This here is Princess," the old man
said, standing as tall as he could. "*He* is
a she, officer. She's my dog. We've been
living together near three months now
and I didn't find her. She found me."

"And what do you have to say about all this, son?" the policeman asked in a kind voice.

I knew this was my chance to get her back. I could tell them everything, and then they'd know who Tina really belonged to. Just then, I heard a bell ringing. I looked up to see a sidewalk Santa moving through the crowd. "Merry Christmas!" he called, swinging his kettle. "Your generosity can help give the needy a very merry Christmas." I could hear the clink of coins dropping into his pot.

I looked at my mom. Her eyes were kind of wet and I think she was thinking the same thing I was. We had each other, and Dad, and Grandma and Grandpa, and a whole family of aunts and uncles and cousins and really good friends. Soon our house would be filled with the smell of good food. The fire would be burning in the fireplace, the tree would be all lit up, and there'd be plenty of noise and fun.

And just before we all started to open our presents, Grandpa would say, like he did every year, "Let's not forget what the true meaning of this season is all about." Then he'd hold up his cup of hot cider and say, "Now let's count our blessings and be grateful that we're able to celebrate together!"

For a minute, I forgot where I was. Then I heard the policeman's voice again. "Well?" he repeated. "What have you got to say, son? Is this your dog?"

Tina and the old man were standing close to each other, looking at me. They both seemed to be waiting for my answer. And that was when I knew. They really did belong together. I couldn't take Tina away. She was the only family the old man had.

"No," I said, "Tina is his dog now."

Mom put her arm around my shoulders and gave me a hug so hard it hurt. "I'm really proud of you," she whispered. "I know how hard that was for you to say."

Someone yelled, "Way to go kid! That's the Christmas spirit."

Suddenly, people started to applaud. I was feeling a lot of things all at once. I felt kind of sad, and I was embarrassed

by all the attention. But I also felt good.
All around me, everyone was smiling.
Especially the old man. He bent down
and came so close to my face, I was
afraid he was going to kiss me.

Instead, he said, "You know that
reward money you talked about?
Now you take that reward money for
yourself, see. Then you go down to
the shelter and pick out another pretty
pup, just the way you picked out the
Princess here. And I'll help you train the
new pup the same way I trained Her
Royal Highness."

He patted Tina on the head again.
She looked up at him and seemed to
smile. There was no doubt about it. Tina
loved the old man as much as he loved

her. And why not? He'd turned her into a princess.

"Sounds like a good idea to me, Zach," Mom said with a smile. "Our family needs a lot of help when it comes to training. I can't even train you to try on a pair of pants."

That made me laugh. My mom could always make me laugh when she really wanted to. "And this way," she went on, "we could give another little orphan a good home."

"But where will we find you?" I asked the old man.

"Easy," he said. "Me and the Princess go to the park every day. You can meet us near the old band shell. Everybody knows me. Just ask for Sam. You can come and visit us anytime you like, and bring along your new pup."

"I've got another idea, Sam," said Mom, with a smile. "Why don't you and

Tina join us and Zach's new puppy for Christmas dinner?"

And that year, and for many years after, that's exactly what they did.

Author's Note

The Christmas Puppy is based on a true story. Several years ago, when our son, Zach, was still in grade school, our family adopted a puppy we named Tina. She was a lively, mischievous little dog who looked just like the puppy in this book. Our Tina also loved to run free, and always found her way home...until the day she pushed open the garden gate and disappeared forever.

We were very sad and searched everywhere for a long time. Finally, we came to accept the fact that Tina wasn't coming back. Like the family in this book, we hoped she had found someone who loved her as much as we did. Maybe someone like Sam, who really needed a good friend.

Still, as time passed, I couldn't help wondering what would happen if we did see Tina again. What if she were happy in her new home? What if her new family wouldn't want to give her back? These thoughts led me to write this story. Knowing Zach's kind heart led me to its conclusion.

Though we never saw our Tina again, we did adopt another abandoned dog. He was as big as Tina was small; as shaggy as she was smooth; as calm as she was frisky...and we loved him every bit as much. I called him The Gentle Giant, though his real name was George—but that's another story.